# Mentoring Matters

## READY, SET, SOAR

*Maureen Bourne Linton and J. Robert Linton*

***Dedicated to the Memory of Ralph Bourne, Meritha Bourne***

***and the***

***Bourne Legacy***

# Mentoring Matters

## READY, SET, SOAR
## Maxine's Story

Maureen Bourne Linton and J. Robert Linton

*Mentoring Matters: Ready, Set Soar – Maxine's Story*
by Maureen F. Bourne Linton and J. Robert Linton
Copyright © 2024 by Maureen F. Bourne Linton and J. Robert Linton
All Rights Reserved.
ISBN: 978-1-59755-789-4

Published by:     ADVANTAGE BOOKS™
                  Orlando, FL
                  www.advbookstore.com

| Library of Congress Catalog Number: 2024941009 | |
|---|---|
| **Names:** | Linton , Maureen F. Bourne and Linton, J. Robert |
| **Title:** | *Mentoring Matters: Ready, Set Soar – Maxine's Story* |
| | Maureen F. Bourne Linton |
| | J. Robert Linton |
| | Advantage Books, 2024 |
| **Identifiers:** | ISBN Paperback: 978159757894 |
| | ISBN eBook: 978159758051 |
| **Subjects:** | |

Cover Design by Jonathan Walker

First Printing: July 2024
24 25 26 27 28 29 30 10 9 8 7 6 5 4 3 2 1

# Table of Contents

# INTRODUCTION

This historical fiction addresses mentoring within a universal framework. The story is set in Jamaica, West Indies, featuring world class athletes from the Caribbean. The journey of Maxine Bennett, a track-and-field enthusiast, and her progress from middle school, age 11 years, through high school, age 18 years. Throughout the plot, fictional stories of the Bennetts of Bell Blossoms, and factual history of the chronicle of track-and-field events and victories of athletes, are skillfully interwoven. The story attempts to demonstrate the effects of mentoring and its impact on the life of students. It skillfully uses the continuous success of prepared athletes and the chronicles of historical sport championships, as motivators in the achievement of academic success.

The story is told through the eyes of Maxine Bennett, a high school student who aspires to become a Pediatric Surgeon. Within this framework, the main character, the resilient Maxine is mentored by Mr. MacLean, a motivational form teacher, along with family, friends and a generous Primary School Principal. While Maxine academically pursues her lifelong dream, her cousins, Marty and Barry, both natural sports enthusiasts and community leaders, powerfully impact her life and inspire her, as they exemplify the value of giving back to the community.

The title *"Ready, Set, Soar"* delineates the focal points of this publication.

*'Readiness,'* is demonstrated in the legendary stories surrounding the student Maxine Bennett, as she prepares for high school entrance, under the mentorship of teacher, Mr. Maclean. The story highlights the results of the students' dedication to disciplined study habits, coupled with the guidance of a mentor, who strengthens her confidence to take the Jamaican, Primary Exit Profile (PEP) exams, which presents the first hurdle of her journey.

'*Set,*' illustrates the support of family, community and life experiences for this journey, while describing the transition of students from elementary to high school.

'*Soar,*' demonstrates Maxine's resilience and the continued support she obtains to make the journey possible. The attributes of being resolute and never whimsically changing her life-long dreams, help her to achieve the next level. 'Soar,' takes place as Maxine is guided to choose the relevant science classes in high school towards fulfilling her mission. Continuous hard work, supported by the motivation gained from victorious athletes enable Maxine to stay focused and make relevant choices, even amid storms and global disasters.

The ongoing success stories of the Jamaican Track-and-Field athletes lay the foundation for Maxine's motivation. Although she is not athletically inclined, there is a parallel between her pursuits and development and the achievements of the athletes over the years.

The authors, Maureen and Robert Linton are inspired to write this book together by merging their interests and life experiences. Maureen, an educator, fully supports the concept of mentoring as the tool to guide students to achieve success. She is convinced that the power of consistent encouragement by a good mentor, leads resilient students to steadfastly pursue and achieve success. Robert, supports the concept and applies the catalyst of motivation, demonstrated through victorious achievements by Jamaican Track and Field athletes. Maxine, the enthusiastic fan, is clearly invigorated and uplifted by the thrill of the results aired, and this helps as she hurdles through levels of intense studies and examinations. The book demonstrates how sports support the building of resilience leading to ultimate success for high achievers. The opportunities to win and lose, lay the framework for building resilience through teamwork and relationship building.

This historical novel takes the reader throughout the land of Jamaica. Maxine's story highlights the contributions of a visionary Premier, Norman Manley who instituted the Common Entrance, an entry level, Jamaican high school examination. It provides insights to the work conducted within two high schools, highlighting the institutions' level of commitment to student success, and a history of Jamaica's contribution to worldwide athletics. The story also provides in depth view of a small Jamaican community, focused on family life and social interactions; and demonstrates the efforts made by a small rural community to deal with the global COVID crisis.

The hallmark of the nation's pivotal moment is also presented through descriptions of cultural celebrations and the annual presentations of festival song competitions; as well as the country's greatest historical achievement of gaining independence from British rule, including the lowering of the British flag and the hoisting of the Jamaican flag followed by the presentation of the new National Anthem. Interwoven in the fabric of this book is the success of athletic heroes including Usain Bolt, Veronica Campbell-Brown, Shelly Anne Frasier-Pryce, Elaine Thompson, Sherika Jackson and hurdlers Omar McLeod and Ainsley Parchment.

*Maureen Bourne Linton and J. Robert Linton*

# PREFACE

SIGNIFICANT HISTORICAL INFLUENCE

Today, as many question why Jamaicans dominate worldwide track-and-field events, the answer might well be found in the historical records of great, athletic ancestors who led with courage. This is alluded to in the section, *"Standing On the Shoulders of Giants."*

Norman Manley, Premiere of Jamaica 1955 to 1961, for example, stands out as one such leader. He was a Rhode Scholar; a graduate of Oxford Law School; and an outstanding Attorney with the legendary reputation of never losing a case. Manley was also an athlete and a natural leader. In the book, *"N.W. Manley and the Making of Modern Jamaica."* (2016). The author, Arnold Bertram, describes the leadership of Norman Manley as a schoolboy.

> " Despite the availability of more senior students, Manley was identified and unanimously chosen for the leadership position of sports captain of Jamaica College. It is said that Norman Manly was automatically elected for leadership positions for the rest of his life by every organization that he joined."

The Editor of *"Jamaica College Magazine"* (1970) wrote.

> "It was most welcome to find a great improvement among the juniors who were a miserable failure last year. Ever since the appointment of Manley as sport captain, there has been regular and systematic training, which led to our coming out of a losing ordeal with a silver trophy."

As Premier of Jamaica in 1959 -1962, Manley introduced the Jamaican Common Entrance Examination, that is replaced by the current Primary Exit Profile (PEP) exams, which lays the foundation for Academic

Education in Jamaica, coupled with the continuation of outstanding sportsmanship within the high schools.

This book tells a story of strong people, great leadership and soaring spirits that lift the country to greatness and inspire students to valiantly move forward and achieve their goals. Maxine's story speaks of a nation of independent thinkers who are willing to unite their efforts and move forward, despite challenges. Even as life events and circumstances dramatically change, and the ravishes of the COVID Virus stealthily plunges the Bell Blossoms community, the nation of Jamaica and the entire world into a fearsome abyss of death and despair, resilience of the human spirit dominates, and the community fights back for survival. Success in education, sports and leadership are outstanding, sustaining factors which enable the nation to take-off at the starter's block, and inspire the writing of this edition," Ready, Set, Soar"

RECOMMENDED TARGET AUDIENCES
- Highschool Students
  - Content suitable for high school students globally
- Mentors and Educational Researchers
  - A highly recommended resource book for mentors and educational researchers, and those who influence the design of curriculums and programs.
- Human interest leisure reading.
  - This historical novel is a delightful human-interest and leisure resource book, as it chronicles the legendary achievements over the years of great sportsmanship It is an endearing, historical keepsake chronicling Jamaican's journey to success through sports, education, independence and strong leadership.

# ACKNOWLEDGEMENTS

Thanks for the loving support of friends and family members who inspired, supported and encouraged us during the process of writing this book. Our acknowledgements include the following:

The technical guidance of Craig Linton, supported by his wife LaKenya, and loving family members, Kingston, Jerrell and Kai; as well as Ryan, Joe, Andrea and Marie Linton; Karen and Jon Walker; Ethan, Caitlyn, and little Kaden, whose unwavering support inspires and uplifts us.

The wise counsel offered by Michelle DaCosta Welsh who constantly remains a friend over many decades.

Editorial insights offered by Sheila Bourne who generously gave of her time to read the book and offer editorial insights, as well as the inspiration of siblings and close family members including Barbara and Richard Grant; Denise & Charles Bridge; Bloom and Karl Wellington; and Woodrow Bourne

The loving guidance of Christopher and Christine Kelman. Thanks to Christopher for his contribution of beautiful photographs of landscapes and nature.

Special thanks to Gregory Tomlinson who stood by us as we navigated cultural borders between US and the Caribbean, and his referral Sheree Rhoden who diligently and professionally led us to negotiate a wide selection of photography.

The contribution of Maurice and Shelley Seville, Yasmin and Garth Holness who reconnected us to a past protégé and gifted artist, Bevon Angus and his delightful renditions of Caribbean paintings.

Thanks to our friend Collin Shaw who is always willing to debate the challenges and celebrate the victory of Jamaican Track and Field stars throughout the years.

*Maureen Bourne Linton and J. Robert Linton*

# CHAPTER 1

# READY – Laying the foundation

> *READY: The runner gets into position.*
> *"On your marks" the Starter yells. The runner focusses on the*
> *track, with feet placed on the block; fingers on the ground behind*
> *the starting line; muscles relaxed.*

## THE BENNETTS OF BELL BLOSSOMS

The sound of keys jingling was like music to Dr. Maxine Bennett-Brown's ears as she carefully locked away the precious stacks of medicines and patients' records before leaving the premises of Bell Blossoms Health Care Center. She smiled as she walked out the doors of the freshly painted building with its beautifully manicured grounds.

After walking a few laps before going home, Maxine felt refreshed as she reflected on all the pediatric patients whom she cared for that day. She prayed earnestly for wisdom to handle each case. Maxine felt like she was walking on air along the quiet hillside, reflecting on her journey as the newlywed, Dr. Maxine Bennett-Brown. She had come a long way, indeed, and she was thankful that she met and married the compassionate medical student, Danny Brown, the love of her life, whom she partnered with, after graduation. While Danny specialized as a General Practitioner, Maxine specialized as a Pediatric Surgeon. She was satisfied that this union helped her to pursue her lifelong dream of establishing the Health Care Center in Bell Blossoms District, Jamaica, West Indies.

Suddenly, the alarm clock rang out, disrupting Maxine's favorite reoccurring dream. She jumped out of bed, missing the opportunity to stop the alarm from going off. As she prepared for the elementary school, Primary Exit Profile (PEP) examinations, for entrance to high school, Maxine practiced waking up at 5.30 am on weekdays to review her work and prepare for daily quizzes. Since she did not like the sound of the alarm, each morning she practiced beating the clock with the hope of becoming an expert at it. Maxine Bennett, lived in Bell Blossoms District, in the Parish of Manchester, and attended Bell Blossoms Elementary School on the Island of Jamaica. Her house was located at the top of a hill, and each morning Maxine was thrilled to see the beautiful sunrise pouring a sparkling yellow glow over the entire village below. She felt invigorated as she watched the graceful swaying of the palm trees in the new light of day.

## A Caribbean Sunrise

COURTESY OF CHRISTOPHER KELMAN

COURTESY OF BEVON ANGUS

Maxine was very excited as she recalled late breaking news just before bedtime the previous night, announcing the tremendous victory of the Jamaican Track and Field Olympic team. The announcement brought back memories of the stories she heard in the village of the 2008 Olympics held in Beijing, China, and the performance of Jamaican athletes Shelley Anne Fraser-Pryce, winner of the gold medal, followed by Sherone Simpson and Kerron Stewart who tied for the silver medal. The performance was dubbed the grand "Sweep," setting a precedence for similar victories over the years. This included the men's 200 meter victory in the London 2012 Olympics, as Usain Bolt captured the gold, Yohan Blake, the silver; and Warren Weir, the bronze medal. These performances helped the island of Jamaica to developed a reputation for consistently producing world-class athletes.

Maxine smiled as she recalled the story of Eldith Andrews, a retired Postal worker, who became famous for announcing the 'Sweep,' over the years. Initially, Eldith delivered telegrams to Bell Blossoms community, however, her position was terminated by the revolution of Online communications, and the proliferation of cellphones, WhatsApp, emails and faxes. Thus, telegram, an added expense to the postal budget became obsolete. This came as a blow to Eldith, the village's self-appointed Town-Cryer, and a previous Telegram bearer who took great pride in her delivery style. Fortunately, Eldith was qualified to take an early retirement from the post office, which she did, then left the employment in a huff.

"Who can shut me down?" she mused.

"I am now an independent woman, and I will continue my great service to the community as I please." Since then, Eldith kept a close ear for urgent news and continued to loudly announce whatever news she gleaned.

The announcement of the victory in 2008 excited Eldith, and it was said that she ran through the village shouting, "Sweep, Sweep.!!" Her strong voice echoed over the hills and valleys of Bell Blossoms, waking up the entire village. Although the good news cheered up the community, the people of Bell Blossoms, were at odds with Eldith because, previously, as a Telegram Bearer, she made it her business to read and announce the contents of each telegram before making the actual delivery.

In the past, neighbors were known to stop in to express condolences, and on one occasion the church bells tolled, to announce a death, even before the family received the telegram. Eldith chose to ignore the protests, therefore, the people were not pleased with her performance. She blissfully carried out her mission, nonetheless.

Marty and Barry Bennett, cousins of Maxine, also lived in Bell Blossoms District. They were outstanding Track and Field enthusiasts who consistently participated in planning celebratory events to commemorate the homecoming victories of Jamaican athletes. Over the years, both cousins became famous for arranging numerous events to host returning athletes and organize transportation for spectators to get to the to the celebration sites. When athletes performed globally and returned to Jamaica, they found the home-coming events especially thrilling; and in their acknowledgements, they mentioned the tremendous support of the Bennett brothers.

During community meetings, Marty and Barry authenticated their stories with displays of large photo albums of pictures taken beside their heroes. Having launched and enhanced their reputation, the Island's Track and Field Association learned of their diligence and came to respect and rely on the ability of the Bennett brothers to bring out the fans and lead the cheers at official gatherings.

Marty and Barry, however, chose to be funded independently and privately and as they rose to prominence; and the National Athletic Leadership of Jamaica respectfully cooperated with their efforts; supported and repeatedly thanked them publicly, in both media broadcasts and newspaper publications. Marty and Barry Bennett were automatically endeared as the cornerstone of the Athletic Welcoming Committee in Jamaica.

Although Maxine had a quiet disposition, she was popular at school because of her connection to the Bennett brothers. Most students referred to her as either Marty or Barry's cousin, which meant that they did not know her name, but she was evidently recognized in the sports community.

Maxine came from a very humble, single-parent home. Her father, Logan Bennett had taken his leave from family responsibilities a long time ago, leaving his wife Myra, a hard-working mother, to take care of the family. Maxine watched over her two siblings Marlene age 4, and Mike age 6, when her mother worked overtime. However, her level of support was strengthened as she could easily call upon her Aunt Angela when needed.

The awareness that her mom suffered from hypertension and the thought of her getting a sudden stroke, not only scared, but mobilized Maxine to skillfully care for Marlene and Mike, in order to alleviate any undue stress on her mother. Aunt Angela and her husband Jim, who lived less than a mile away from the Bennett's home, were very responsive to the needs of Maxine's family. Angela was Myra's last sibling, and she was deeply offended by thoughts of the hurt inflicted on her sister by her estranged husband, Logan Bennett. She feared the added stress could give her hypertensive-ridden sister a stroke; therefore, Angela and Jim stayed fully attentive to Myra's family in every conceivable way.

Maxine knew very little about her father, Logan Bennett, except that he went away to America and never returned to Jamaica when she was younger. She gathered from Myra that initially he sent money back, along with barrels of food and clothing. However, his gifts gradually decreased, and after a few years he stopped sending altogether. Since no one heard from Logan Bennett, Myra lost all track of his existence. She survived as a diligent and independent woman, and she was quite satisfied with Angela and Jim's devotions to her family; Marlene and Mike's temperate, easy-going personalities and the support they offered her and Maxine.

While Angela and Jim had no children of their own, they maintained a very stable marriage, and found it relatively simple to watch over the Bennett's household. When Jim was present, the children listened to, and followed his instructions, and this made life so much easier and peaceful for both families. Even though Jim's personality was non-threatening, he had an authoritative father-figure presence, which the children respectfully responded to.

However, Myra and Angela sometimes found his ease-of-command irksome, as their attempts at disciplining the children were clearly less effective. The ladies wondered why the children did not respond to them in the way they did to Jim. It did not matter how loud or threatening they got, it made no difference in the way the children responded to them. Although this factor remained a mystery, the ladies admitted that it added a well-needed dimension to foster the stability of both families and therefore, they gave Jim their full support.

While Maxine diligently cared for her mother and siblings, she dreamed of one day becoming a Pediatric Surgeon, a decision she was embarrassed to share in her small community. She feared being labelled a lofty dreamer, as the idea of finding money to even attempt to pursue such a career seemed impossible. In addition to the dilemma her family faced, Maxine had seen enough undernourished and totally underprivileged children in the community to strengthen her resolve to have influence and strive to build a career to save the lives of children.

## GUIDED BY A MENTOR, MOTIVATED BY ATHLETES

Maxine's love for track-and-field was reinforced by her mentor, Mr. Maclean, a past student of Kings High. As the six grade students prepared for transition to high school, they were scheduled weekly to meet with mentors. This new program was well embraced by Maxine's peers and each week they excitedly looked forward to the stories and encouragement they received from the program.

Mr. Maclean chose to mentor his protégés as young leaders. He spoke very openly about his high school experiences at Kings High School, as his early years at Kings had a profound impact on his life and leadership abilities. Today, Kings continues to be a popular school known for excellence in leadership and sporting activities, especially in Track and Field.

The students understood and respected his role, as he took time to carefully explain the history of mentorship and its lasting results when conducted well. He related the ancient story carried by Fabisch (2005).

> *"In Greek Mythology "Odysseus appoints an old friend, Mentor, to watch over his household and son, Telemachus, in his absence during the Trojan War. By nearly all accounts Mentor was a protective, guiding and supportive figure who acted as a wise and trusted counselor to Telemachus, son of Odysseus. The story was passed on to other generations, because of Mentor's relationship with*

> *Telemachus, and the encouragement and practical plans he was taught to deal with personal dilemmas. The name 'Mentor' has been adopted in Latin and other languages, including English, as a term meaning someone who imparts wisdom to, and shares knowledge with a less-experienced colleague."*

According to Rhodes (2001)

> *"The first recorded modern usage of the term can be traced to a 1699 book entitled 'Les Aventures de Télémaque' by the French writer François Fénelon. In the book, the lead character is Mentor. This book was very popular during the 18th century and the modern application of the term can be traced to this publication."*

Mr. Maclean embraced the motto of King's High, his Alma Mater *"Never yield, never give up."* He led rigorous discussions on athletic performances and told the life stories of the ladies in the "Sweep," revealing the dogma they applied to stick with the sport, until they got to the very top. Mr. Maclean also discussed other Jamaican sport heroes such as Veronica Campbell Brown, and the legendary Usain Bolt.

Maxine was excited, as she too strove for excellence and felt the comradery with others who did. He described the lives of the athletes; their communities; what inspired them to greatness; how they conquered adversities; and how they related to others when they became winners. These stories strengthened Maxine's resolve to excel in her chosen career and motivated her to firmly believed that just like her favorite athletes, she too would rise to prominence in whatever professional field she chose to pursue.

## TRANSITIONING TO HIGH SCHOOL

As the semester ended, it occurred to Maxine that she was the only student who did not know for sure what high school she would choose to attend if she passed the PEP examination. During mentoring sessions, guided by Mr. Maclean, she searched the Nation's List of '*Best High Schools.*' Maxine noted that city schools such as Kensington and St. Johns High, consistently carried top ratings. Placements or ranks were based on the graduation rate of students who passed five (5) or more subjects in the Caribbean Secondary Education Certificate (CSEC), school leaving examinations. Many of such schools were located in far-away, inaccessible places such as Kingston and St. Andrews.

Maxine was resolute and remained undaunted by the results. Her persistent research finally yielded Kent High; a boarding school located an hour away from home. Kent ranked within the top 10 high schools nationwide, in academic areas. Maxine was pleased to uncovered that although Kent was known for limited participation in sports activities, the school showed excellence in academics, and was highly rated and respected nationally.

Maxine felt that a neighboring boarding school would afford her time to focus on studies yet keep her within proximity to home in case she was needed urgently. Trusting the help and encouragement of her aunt and uncle, Maxine confidently made a decision that would enhance her motivation to get top scores on the PEP.

Above all, Kent High was Aunt Angela's alma mater. She was delighted to hear of Maxine's choice and shared all she knew about her beloved school. Maxine was motivated by the profound knowledge of the history and foundation of Kent High. She confidently felt that these factors would enable her to get off to a great start and fit in well. She had heard enough from Aunt Angela to set her heart ablaze with excitement.

Earlier, Maxine wrestled with the decision of whether to study during the Independence holidays or celebrate. Finally, she decided to take time off to do the latter, as she recalled previous experiences which led her to conclude that disrupted studies were unproductive. However, when the week of the publication of the PEP examination results arrived, she hoped she had made the right decision.

Maxine along with all the young scholars on the island of Jamaica waited with baited breaths to get copies of the local newspapers. Maxine got up early and dressed, to await the newspaper drop-off at a local shop.

She had stayed awake the previous night, anxiously replaying in her head all the responses she wrote on the examination paper. Although she was satisfied with her answers, she also had misgivings, as she was aware of the stiff competition. She knew that many gifted applicants competed for the award, regardless of very few coveted spaces in the high schools throughout the island.

Maxine struggled to suppress all the *'what ifs'* that popped into her mind. Doubts were obstacles she had been taught to avoid, so like a true champion, she mustered the courage to open the newspaper. Yes, her name appeared boldly, and she was awarded a full scholarship for the school of her dreams, Kent High. This meant that almost all expenses would be covered for her future education. Maxine felt she was floating on wings of eagles as she ran home to break the news to her family.

# IMAGES OF VICTORIOUS ATHLETES

## Donald Quarrie: Montreal Olympics 1976 with Herb McKenley

COURTESY OF JAMAICA GLEANER

## MERLENE OTTEY: Sprint Legend, 2013

COURTESY OF JAMAICA GLEANER

**Usain Bolt: Olympics 2016, Rio, Brazil**

COURTESY OF JAMAICA GLEANER

# Chapter 2

# SET: Life Events Influence Maturity

*The Starter yells "Get Set"*
*The runner raises the hips slightly above shoulder level; feet pushed hard into the blocks; holding breath...*

## CRISIS HANDLED BY A CARING COMMUNITY

The bright, flashing lights of an ambulance caught Maxine's attention as she approached home. Looking closer, Maxine identified her mom being transported on a stretcher towards an ambulance parked in her driveway. Maxine felt faint as her heightened emotions suddenly plummeted. She feared that her mom had suffered a severe stroke; the reality she dreaded most, for the past few years. This was Maxine's watershed moment.

The next few weeks were blurry in her consciousness as she battled to stay focused while juggling the management of her household; visits to the hospital; and care for her mom. Maxine wondered if her new conquest of attaining the scholarship would survive this emotional upheaval. Thankfully, the semester was ending and the summer break would give her time to focus on matters at hand.

The community was aware of the Bennett's crisis, and the cousins, Marty & Barry, ever watchful and caring for Maxine's welfare, busily drummed up all the support needed to override the crisis. Teams from the neighborhood were skillfully maneuvered to drop off freshly cooked meals daily and pick up clothes to be laundered. The neighborhood church also helped with child-care matters by sending teams from the Youth Group to stop by the Bennett's verandah periodically; care for the children; and to engage them in play.

One day, Maxine heard an urgent wrap on her door. When she opened the door, she was at a loss for words when she saw her Principal at the door. Nervous and quite shaken, Maxine expected the worst. However, Principal Jones heartily congratulated her for the stellar achievement of the Scholarship she received. Principal Jones then proceeded to hand Maxine a letter. She read a portion that left her speechless. The letter came from an anonymous group of Jamaican Athletes who became aware of the dilemmas she faced, including caring for her mother, and simultaneously facing the decision of going away to board at Kent High. A section of the principal's letter read:

> ..... *"Congratulations on receiving the Annual award for best all-island scholastic achievements in the PEP Examinations. Your consistent participation in hosting athletic fans on your verandah to benefit the entire community of Bell Blossoms; and your family members' unwavering passion to support track-and-field events, have not gone unnoticed. This scholarship is awarded to you by the Government of Jamaica, via the Ministry of Education, to the student who scores the highest grades in the recent PEP Examinations. Having researched your background and current set of circumstances, this group of anonymous Jamaican World Class athletes understands that the tragic illness of your mother would make it impossible for you to take advantage of the scholarship. Therefore, it gives us immense pleasure to offer you the following additional awards to ensure that you will be able to take full advantage of this very prestigious and well-deserved opportunity.*
>
> *Funds will be made available annually, for the duration of 5 years, to provide your full support through high school. Additionally, on a long-term basis, funds will be provided*

*for the care of your mother, including the daily provision of a nurse and also household help for the care of the children.*

*Individual offers will be made to your cousins, Marty and Barry as we are forever grateful for their unwavering support."* .....

Maxine's joy was complete. At that moment, she understood that her vision of one day becoming a Pediatric Surgeon was no longer a dream. With financial support in place, she could begin her journey by majoring in relevant science courses at high school level. She pledged to do her very best to make her donors proud of the generous contributions she received.

Within Maxine's heart, she knew that seeds of greatness had been planted, and watered. Finally, they had blossomed with the help of the generosity of the Athletic Association; the love and support of the community of friends on the verandah; and the ongoing stories of outstanding athletes who motivated her as they consistently blazed pathways to victory, regardless of their circumstances. Maxine felt like an athlete crouching at the starter block. At this point, she was ready. High school, her next hurdle was being set up and reinforced by generosity. In her heart, she was confident that one day she would truly soar.

## MOTIVATIONAL IMAGES OF A BEAUTIFUL HOMELAND KEEPS MAXINE GOAL ORIENTED AND FOCUSED

COURTESY OF BEVON ANGUS

COURTESY OF CHRISTOPHER KELMAN

*Maureen Bourne Linton and J. Robert Linton*

COURTESY OF MAUREEN LINTON

## KENT HIGH: Orientations,

## Global Traditions, and the Mentoring Factor

From Aunt Angela's recollection of the early sixties, Kent High hosted about 60% international students per year. However, Maxine noted that in 2020, the numbers fell as the institution continued to host between 20-25% international students and provide dormitory accommodations for both local and foreign boarders. Kent High students, smartly dressed in combined olive-green and white tunics, represented the institution well.

Teachers and administrators across the globe, and locally, are also housed on campus. When Maxine enrolled, the full campus accommodated the following sections: pre-kindergarten, kindergarten, junior high school, high school, and a Community College. On a daily basis, the school bussed students from the neighboring parishes of Manchester, Clarendon, St. Ann, and Trelawny.

Aunt Angela recalled that as a new student, she was initially awed by the vastness of Kent High's landscape. It took her awhile to fully comprehend the extent of the education she was exposed to, and she felt deep appreciation as the experience expanded her horizons, not only academically, but in her understanding of how the world works.

During the first week of orientation, Maxine gathered that Kent High, was founded by Gregory Sullivan of Boston, Massachusetts and Adam Brown of Jamaica. Sullivan, an Anglican Pastor and Brown a Businessman, purchased lands in the hills of St. Ann, close to the border of Manchester.

During the excitement of the first few days at school, surrounded by all the new faces, Maxine had to try hard to stay focused. Her reassurance came from reflections on Mr. MacLean's mentoring sessions, and thoughts of earlier days and friendships at Bell Blossoms elementary kept her calm, as she navigated the new environment. Mr. Maclean believed she would make it, and this gave her the courage to face new challenges.

Throughout the first few weeks of school, students were anxious and demanded to see the homeroom teacher for every incident. Maxine's homeroom teacher, Miss Dean, focused mostly on clarifying directions for the 20 students in homeroom, as each student had slight variations within their daily schedules, and they were mostly anxious about getting lost. The thought of scrambling to find new classrooms every 45 minutes when the bell rang, was definitely scary for the new students. In time they calmed down, and Miss Dean's role broadened. She became indispensable to all, as she made herself available to resolve the problem of each student.

Maxine sat between Wendy Adams and Karen Carter. The three girls immediately compared schedules, discovered they all had similar classes the first few days, and they immediately bonded. Maxine was thankful for her last name, Bennett. This meant she was advantageously positioned alphabetically in activity line-ups, and placements. During the first few weeks of school all new students vied for positions in choosing extracurricular activities.

Some days however, her schedule did not line-up with Wendy and Karen's, and unfortunately, she got lost one Friday, making her way from the cafeteria to the science lab building. Leaving the cafeteria, she confidently identified all the buildings along the way, including the male dormitory, some staff houses, the gymnasium, some classrooms, the language laboratory, tuck shop, the music studio, library, the campus administrative building and the chapel. Stopping by her locker which was located along the corridor outside the English department, Maxine had to muscle her way through the crowd to find it, as the students rushed to lockers to pick up books before the next bell rang.

She paused before heading in the direction of the General Science Laboratory, which appeared on her daily schedule, as she struggled to master a new combination lock, which took her a while to figure out.

Feeling confused after getting caught up in the swirl of activities around her, Maxine ran ahead to join a group of students whom she had seen previously in her classroom. Unfortunately, they all entered the mathematics room, leaving her to pause for a second time, to examine her schedule. After wandering around for a few more minutes, the bell rang, and the corridors were almost cleared. Feeling really lost, Maxine sat on a wall to catch her bearings. She took out the map, which was distributed during the first week of school, to help students locate their destinations. General Science was located in another block of the buildings, across the quadrangle where she rested.

Thoughts of late detention caused her to sweat profusely. Thankfully, Annie, a senior hall monitor, stopped by and kindly offered to escort her to class. Annie explained that she was not alone, as many new students needed help at the beginning of the school year. To her relief, the teacher merely nodded at her to take a seat, without giving the written warning she expected. Maxine, never wanting to repeat that painful ordeal, practiced to pay full attention to minute details, especially details of the campus layout.

## THE SCHOOL LIBRARY

The discovery of the school library was a pivotal and lifechanging experience for Maxine. She had never before seen such a large collection of books in one room, and her mind raced as she thought of the amount of information she could glean from such a place. She was impressed by the deep silence that permeated the room, and the focused look on the faces of students, busily researching topics.

Although Maxine had not yet received assignments for library research, she decided to research her favorite topic, which was 'Athletics.' With the help of the librarian, Maxine uncovered a wealth of information, leading her to conclude that her favorite athletes were standing on the shoulders of greater athletes. Maxine entitled her paper:

## ON THE SHOULDERS OF GIANTS:

### The Early History Of Jamaican Track And Field

> *After the 1938 Olympics in Munich, Germany there were no more Summer Olympics until The London games in 1948. Jamaica sent a team, which included Herb McKenley, Les Laing, George Roden and Arthur Wint. Wint won the Silver medal in the 800 meters and the gold medal in the 400 meters; Herb McKenley won the 400 meters silver medal.*

*Again, Jamaica had good success in the 1952 Summer games in Helsinki, Finland, as Mckinley won the silver medal in the 100 meters; George Roden won the 400 meters race in a new Olympic record time of 45.9; and Mckenley won the Silver medal. The team of Les Laing, George Roden, Arthur Wint and Herb McKenley won gold medals in the 4 x 400 meters relay in the record time of 3 minutes 3.9 seconds.*

*Jamaica did not win any Olympics medal in 1956, 1960, 1964. However, in the 1968 Olympics held in Mexico City, Lennox Miller won a silver medal in the 100 meters race. In 1972 he won a bronze medal in the 100 meters race in Munich, Germany. In 1976, Don Quarrie struck gold in the 200 meters race in Montreal Olympics, and he also won the silver medal in the 100 meters race.*

*During the period of 1980 to 2000, Merlene Ottey, a great Jamaican sprinter dominated as a female sprinter. She represented Jamaica in 8 Olympics and many world championships, with great success. She won 9 Olympic medals, including 3 silver and 6 bronze medals. Ottey also won 14 World Championships, including 3 gold, 4 silver, and 7 bronze medals.*

*Other notable women sprinters during this period were Juliet Cuthbert who won 2 silver medals in Barcelona, Spain Olympics in 1992; Grace Jackson won a silver medal in the Seoul, Japan Olympics in 1988; and in the Atlanta, Georgia summer Olympics of 1996, Deon Hemmings won the 400 meters hurdle, gold medal; while Merlene Ottey won silver in both the 100 meters and the 200 meters. Melaine Walker won the gold in 400 meters hurdle in the Beijing Olympics of 2008*

## HISTORICAL IMAGES OF OUTSTANDING
## TRACK AND FIELD VICTORS

(c) 1962 The Gleaner Co. (Media) Ltd.

COURTESY OF THE JAMAICA GLEANER

**Dr. Arthur Wint, carrying the torch at the 9th Central American and Caribbean Games during the lap of honor on the opening night of the games on August 25, 1962. From left are George Rhoden, Les Laing and Herbert McKenley. Dr Wint was a member of the Jamaican relay team which broke the World record at the Olympic Games in Helsinki**

**1948 - George Rhoden running at the Marlie race track Old Harbour. Rhoden went on to set the world record in 400m race at the Olympic Games in Helsinki, Finland in 1952.**

COURTESY OF THE JAMAICA GLEANER

(c) 2006 The Gleaner Co. (Media) Ltd.

**Herb McKenley examines token presented to him by residents of cluster 3 of the Rex Nettleford Hall on the U.W.I Campus shortly after it was renamed the Herb McKenley Cluster.**

COURTESY OF THE JAMAICA GLEANER

(c) The Gleaner Co, (Media) Ltd.

**1964 - Lennox Miller competed in the Penn Relays in 1964, a week after the North Street based - school, Kingston College, had one the annual Boys' Championships for a third consecutive year.**

COURTESY OF THE JAMICA GLEANER

The Librarian was impressed by the findings of a first form student, in her first semester of high school. She insisted that Maxine's work should be published and guided her to make a guest presentation at the afterschool

Literary Club. Maxine was amazed at the thunderous applause she received at the end of her presentation. Word got around campus really fast, and by the end of the week she recalled getting many congratulatory comments, thumbs up, nods and smiles as she walked across campus. Maxine was thrilled.

As the semester ended and grades were posted, Maxine, along with everyone else, studied the performance of classmates. Her grades were excellent, and she noticed that Karen and Wendy grades were equally as good. Kent High used a Grade Point Average (GPA) system, based on cumulative grades, and students were required to complete a portfolio of work, and received grades based on projects, quizzes, mid and end of semester tests, as well as final year examinations.

Unfortunately, the public posting of grades also exposed the results of weaker students. Although it was intended to motivate them to strive for excellence, it in fact, caused much embarrassment. Maxine happened to noticed the low grades of Michael, an Irish student who entered campus as a boarder, two weeks after the beginning of the semester. She was concerned, as it was shocking to see that he was clearly failing.

One evening, Maxine sat at dinner in the cafeteria with Michael and other students. An upperclassman at the table grilled him about his late arrival on campus, and Michael revealed that all was not well at home. His parents had a bitter divorce, and he was sent off to boarding school in Jamaica. His downcast and nonchalant attitude stood out. Maxine had seen him on campus, and also in her homeroom sessions in the mornings, and she concluded that he was always distracted, or daydreaming. However, she had also seen him at track and field try-outs in PE classes and he was, by far, the faster runner in the first form. It amazed her to know that family problems could affect Michael's ability to study, and severely impact his grades. After discussing Michael's issues with Karen and Wendy, the three girls planned to help him.

It was well known that falling below a GPA of 2.0, by the end of a school year raised a red flag, and the scholarships of such students were rescinded. Such students received a series of warning notices, as well as chances to meet with mentors in various subject areas. However, failure meant that failing students had to transfer to other schools.

Maxine and her friends decided to support Michael when he ran his races in the next PE class. They knew that his failure could be averted if he requested additional work and took advantage of available coaching and mentoring services on campus. Therefore, they cheered him on and encouraged him to give serious consideration to pursue Track and Field. Michael was willing to give it some thought, and Mr. Clintock, the coach, joined in the conversation. Coach was also a very popular mentor at Kent High, and he became quite engaged in the conversation.

The girls were ecstatic when Coach Clintock offered to assist Michael with coaching and mentoring. Maxine and her friends were pleased to learn that Michael followed up and made an appointment to meet with the coach.

Later, grade postings revealed that Michael's grades had improved and he was no longer in danger of losing his scholarship. The incident reminded Maxine of the diligence of her mentor, Mr. Maclean and his influence on her personal development. She felt confident that linking Michael with a mentor was the right thing to do.

During homeroom session, at the end of the first semester, the classmates excitedly disclosed their progress and victories. They were vibrant, competitive and willing to take full advantage of the wide selection of extracurricular activities offered. Maxine joined the debating club and participated in an all-island competition. She hoped to continue, and to get opportunities to travel with the team to other competitions held in high schools across Jamaica. Both Karen and Wendy were passionate about swimming and received awards at the end-of-semester prizegiving ceremony. Students excelled in a wide range of activities including soccer, hockey, javelin, rugby, tennis, netball, volleyball, basketball, swimming, track and field, debating and music.

Legendary stories from the past continued to circulate on campus. Many came from the mixed population of the 70s, when Kent High population was 60% local students and 40% foreign students. One well-known story circulated about a summer camp misadventure, attended by students from the North Pole region of Alaska. Although Kent High is located in one of the coolest regions of Jamaica, in the hills of St. Ann, the temperature was not cold enough for the students to make an adjustment, so they were quickly flown back to the North Pole. Before departing, however, they took part in building the local community basic school. Students habitually wrote their names in the wet cement, and today, the North Pole students names are still engraved at the base of the basic school building.

Other influential foreign features included the celebration of festivities such as Thanksgiving dinners, Valentine and barn dances, which were hosted to give students from around the world opportunities to experience insights to other cultures.

Guy Fawkes Day was the strangest celebration of all, and it gave insight to the United Kingdom's (UK) culture. On November 5th, the UK's Bonfire Night, also known in the UK as Guy Fawkes Night (or Guy Fawkes Day) was celebrated.

According to Online magazine, *"National Today"*, "This holiday marked the failed attempts in the 17th century, to blow up Britain's Parliament and assassinate King James I." To commemorate the occasion, a few safe bon fires were lit across Kent High campus, causing much excitement and generating a lot of tall tales.

## KENT HIGH WORK-STUDY PROGRAM

Besides having unique exposure to different cultures, Kent High was known for Work-Study, a program developed to introduce students to a wholesome lifestyle. It was geared to build effective work ethics, and provide work experience, as students had the opportunity to work on the projects that complement their career choices.

This program was fully supervised by faculty members, and senior students were required to complete a practical project for a few hours weekly. The final portfolio included tasks such as caring for animals, planting vegetables; teaching at the on-campus community basic school; working in science labs or music studio. As this was a novel concept to Jamaican high school education, visitors from other educational institutions were welcomed to tour the campus.

Maxine was intrigued about a story she heard of a group of boys who were warned not to visit the farm to see the arrival of new cows. This piqued the boys' interest, and they sneaked out of class, to see the unloading of the cows from the trucks. However, the principal, knowing their strong curiosity stood at the farm and waited for them. It is said that they were all suspended, while others reported that warning letters were sent home to their parents and copied onto their files. This exercise, however, set the tone for the firm discipline that was demanded for participating in that program.

## SUMMER VACATION AT BELL BLOSSOMS

Maxine returned home for the summer vacation, brimming with stories which she shared with her family and friends. Thankfully, all went well at home and her mother, under the watchful care of Aunt Angela and family, showed much improvement. The family was pleased with Maxine's first report card and openly praised her efforts. Marty and Barry joined in the celebrations and gave her a gift of fifty dollars (US$50) to start a savings account. It was a beautiful homecoming treat.

Summer track-and-field competitions were underway and Maxine and other past students returned to Bell Blossoms Elementary, the beloved alma mater, to watch the events. That summer, Bell Blossoms Elementary was selected to host the Annual Regional Sports Day. The location was perfect as the property had acres of well-trimmed grounds to host all the activities. This was a very prestigious event and many areas high schools participated.

Tremendous excitement and an outpouring of comments came from neighboring Vere Technical, Manchester High, and Holmwood Technical High students, as they touted past sports day glories. They boasted of alumni such as Sherika Jackson of Vere Technical and Elaine Thompson of Manchester High.

Larger-than-life images were posted to intimidate and discourage contenders hoping to win medals. This strategy was substantial, as annually, area high schools vied for bragging rights to out-class other local competitors. The power of success was undeniably strong and regional schools had to fight doubly hard to stay in the competition.

The participants were happy to know that they were not required to contend with athletes from Usain Bolt's school in Cornwall County. Thankfully, Cornwall competed in a separate zone, otherwise, the pressure would be unbearable. '*Usain Bolt, living legend, fastest man on the planet,*' whose name was virtually on the tip of every tongue, presented real psychological challenges to the athletes.

The participants could clearly recall similar historical victories when psychological strategies were effectively used to combat the opponents of the great Muhammed Ali, a US boxer of yesteryear, and master of Psychological Warfare. The strategy was just as effective when Bolt's name was applied to local competitions in the Track and Field arena.

Historically, Sports Day activities were scheduled on separate days for each region, therefore, well-known Sports figures were known to show up unannounced, to lend support to young athletes in their division.

Periodically, the heads of the over-enthusiastic Bennett brothers could be spotted, bobbing through the crowds and many false alarms went off declaring sightings of real stars.

As Maxine busied herself serving in the sandwich line, she happened to look up at the person she served. Her 4-feet, 7th grader height, limited her vision, so she had to look way-up-high. Maxine stared into the steady gaze of Usain Bolt himself. She almost fainted. Mr. Bolt calmly reassured her.

> *"Carry on he said, you are doing a great job. I know who you are Maxine, and I really want to thank you for the paper you wrote on 'Standing on Giant Shoulders.' Maxine, I am inspired by your findings. It helps me to strive to be a better example for those who come behind."*

The rest of the day went by as a blur for Maxine. She floated around with the biggest smile on her face.

## THE PASSION: JAMAICAN SUMMERTIME CELEBRATIONS

Summertime in Jamaica was marked by many outstanding celebrations. At the end of the school year graduates actively hunted for jobs; prepared for transitions such as high schools or colleges; some helped parents in family businesses; or even stayed at home and cared for siblings while parents with significant jobs went to worked.

Summer Olympics events were celebrated universally, and across the island, much attention was paid to other aired events such as the High

School Championship Games (CHAMPS), swimming, tennis and cricket. Non-athletic events included Caribbean Carnivals, Reggae concerts and the Jamaican Independence Celebrations.

The Bennet's verandah was the community gathering place for notable global and local events, and a large, flat-screen television was brought out on such occasions. The engaging Bennett brothers never failed to educate the good people of Bell Blossoms district on updated status in track-and-field, their favorite sport. The discussions were enthusiastic and animated. In time the entire community looked forward to the gathering on Maxine's verandah, made popular by Barry and Marty Bennett. Such gatherings brought back memories of the 1988 Jamaican Bobsled race when the people gathered in a similar style, in many districts throughout the island and enthusiastically cheered the team on. This event subsequently inspired the compelling drama, 'Cool Runnings,' a box office blitz which made over $243.4 US millions, globally.

Maxine was told that the Jamaica Bobsled event of Calgary Canada 1988 attracted one of the largest gatherings on the verandah. However, the enthusiasm was rivaled by the gathering on Maxine's verandah, to celebrate Usain Bolt's victories, in the men's 100 & 200-meters, won in record time at the 2008 Olympics in Beijing, China.

## THE BOLT FACTOR

The name Usain Bolt and its connection to lightning bolt, an appropriate name for the fastest man on the planet seems more than coincidental, and many wondered if his role was preordained.

COURTESY OF THE JAMAICA GLEANER
**Usain Bolt: Iconic pose "To the World."**

In 2009, Bolt broke both world records which he had set in Beijing the previous year at the World Championship held in Berlin, Germany. Bolt lowered the 100-meter timing to 9.58 seconds and the 200-meter to 19.19 seconds. In the Rio Olympics in 2016, Bolt won both gold medals consecutively. His stellar performances shocked the world, and Usain Bolt was enshrined as the fastest man on the planet.

## GLEN MILLS: MENTOR 'PAR EXCELLENCE'

Marty explained to the people on the verandah that historically, it was reported that at the age of 20, Bolt asked his coach, Glen Mills what would it take to become a legend? Coach Mills told Bolt that the winner of gold medals in three consecutive Olympics would certainly grant him legendary status. This answer became Bolts guiding star and the cornerstone of his success. The folks on the verandah celebrated in awe, inspired by Bolt and his great Coach, Glen Mills.

COURTESY OF THE JAMAICA GLEANER

**Glen Mills, past high school coach, receives medal of honor from Camperdown High, 2012**

COURTESY OF THE JAMAICA GLEANER

**Glen Mill congratulated by Prime Minister Portia Simpson Miller at the Heroes Day awards ceremony held on the lawns of Kings House on Monday October 20, 2014**

Mills writes in his testimonial, taken from the book, *"Usain Bolt, The Fastest Man Alive, (2016) p101."*:

> *"My attitude towards coaching is not one-dimensional, it is also geared towards acquiring life skills. From that standpoint, whoever I've trained, I've tried to get them to understand the skills and values in life so that they not only fulfill their potential as athletes but are also balanced people. My philosophy is that you can reach them so much better if you come across not just as their teacher but as their friend."*

## HOMECOMING, 2008

The animated cousins graphically recounted the story of an earlier experience related to their trip to the airport, in 2008, to see the triumphant arrival of Bolt as he returned to Jamaica. It was almost impossible to get a glimpse of Bolt's head towering over the massive crowd.

However, the Bennetts gathered from the excited chatter of the crowd, that Bolt was headed for the Pegasus Hotel in New Kingston. With a determination to beat the crowds, the young, agile Bennett boys dashed out of the airport at lightning speed. Predicting that his entourage would take the Mountain View Road to the hotel, they took the shorter route through Vineyard Town, then sped up South Camp Road, which was traffic-free all the way. Breathlessly, they arrived at the Pegasus and entered the lobby just before the doors were secured for Bolt's protected entrance. Hearts raced as they got a real close-up look at the magnificent athlete.

The Bennett's recounted how one man in the crowd proudly and loudly declared that Mr. Bolt was a wealthy man, valuing maybe a million dollars. This gentleman did not understand the worth of his great victories, the 2009 win of the 200 meters in 19.19 seconds in Berlin Germany; or 100 meters in 9.58 seconds at the world championship in Germany, both new world records; and again, winning both gold medals in the Rio Olympics in 2016. The proud gentleman did not grasp that Bolt's 2021 net worth would be valued millions. Mr. Bolt's value also included his eight-time Olympic gold medalist achievement, currently holding the world record for 100 meters in 9.58 seconds.

Meanwhile, the people cheered as Bolt, a truly warm-spirited young man with an engaging smile, visibly awed the crowd as he responded with his signature move, "To the World." It was a memorable night, and the cousins told it well, as they engaged the entire gathering on the stoop, in rapt attention.

Marty and Barry vividly described other athletes who were also celebrated in 2008 including Shelley Anne Fraser-Pryce, who won the gold and Sherone Simpson and Kerron Stewart who tied for the silver medal. Veronica Campbell-Brown won 200 meters gold medal and Melaine Walker won the 400 meters hurdles at the Olympics in Beijing, China.

Tales of the victories of prominent Track & Field victors were never lacking. As the evenings wore on, the brothers regaled their audience with stories of other outstanding athletes including Veronica Campbell Brown and Hurdler, Ansel Parchment.

## ODE TO VERONICA CAMPBELL BROWN

The story of Veronica Campbell-Brown, who arrived in Jamaica at the same time as Bolt in 2008, was also related by the Bennett brothers. Veronica was introduced as, winner of the women's 200 meters in Beijing, retaining her title from the 2004 women's 200 meters in Athens. On the day following Bolt's arrival, both cousins drove all the way to Sam Sharp Square in Montego Bay to attend the celebrations and grand motorcade held for all the athletes.

(c) 2011 The Gleaner Co. (Media) Ltd.

COURTESY OF THE JAMAICA GLEANER
**Veronica Campbell - 2011 World Championship Athletics, Daegu, South Korea**

Maxine listened carefully as the cousins related stories of the celebrated Veronica Campbell Brown. She was born in Clarks Town Trelawny and had nine siblings. Before going to the University of Arkansas in the US, she attended Vere Technical school in Clarendon. Maxine was inspired as she understood the local school system, and she related well to insights of the journey taken by Veronica to achieve greatness.

The highly elated cousins impressively reeled off stats describing the great achievements over the years, of Veronica Campbell Brown, who ranked all-time top ten position in the world for 100 and 200 meters. Campbell continues to rank top-10 among Jamaican female athletes, with a personal best of 10.76 seconds in the women's 100 meters. Also, in the women's 200 meter, her winning time of 21.74 seconds ranked her in the all-time top-10 in the world. The boys were emotional as they made the declaration that Veronica earned a total of 46 medals in her grand career, with a total of: 27 gold, 16 silver, 3 bronze medals. They recounted emphatically that Veronica cried at the presentation service when the Jamaican flag was hoisted, and the National Anthem was played at Sam Sharpe Square in Montego Bay. This brought back memories of the tears she previously shed, when the Jamaica National Anthem was played at Athens, Greece award ceremony, when she received the 200 meters gold medal.

## HURDLING: A NOTEWORTHY FIELD EVENT

In 2016, Hurdler Omar McLeod won a gold medal in 110 meters hurdles at the Olympics in Rio. McLeod was the first Jamaican to achieve this fete.

**Hurdler, Hansle Parchment and his Demonstration of *'The Brotherhood Of Man'***

COURTESY OF THE JAMAICA GLEANER

**Hurdler, Hansle Parchment celebrating his gold medal**

For decades, the historical landmark case of Jessie Owens vs Adolph Hitler, 1935 served to reflect a disdainful period of racism in global Olympics. However, current prevailing emphases on the strategies of racial diversity and equity, bring new challenges, and demand individual accountabilities. Jamaicans, known for their sense of national pride, are guided by the motto, "Out of Many One People." This was demonstrated by the actions of Hansel Parchment, the Jamaican Hurdler in Tokyo Japan, and endorsed by the immediate response of the Government of Jamaica. The heartwarming story demonstrating generosity of spirit displayed by one athlete and, its far-reaching effects captured the attention of over 1.38 million viewers on social media, and made headlines in Japan and abroad. The Bennett Boys shared the following story taken from "*The Business Insider,*" India (2021) with a gathering on the Verandah:

> *"The Jamaican hurdler Hansle Parchment won gold in the men's 110-meter hurdles at the Tokyo Olympics. He nearly missed the semi-final race after taking the wrong bus, but a volunteer gave him cab money. After the race, Parchment tracked down the woman, Tijana Stojkovic, to thank her and offer gifts. Parchment literally retraced his steps to find Stojkovic and thanked her for her help. Two days after the race, Parchment posted a video to Twitter - which was later reshared by Jamaican Prime Minister Andrew Holness.*
>
> *The video shows Parchment finding Stojkovic at a bus stop, expressing his gratitude to her, and actually saying, "You were instrumental in getting me to the finals that day." Parchment then showed Stojkovic his Gold Medal; gifted her with a yellow Team Jamaica shirt; and refunded the cab fare. The pair then posed for a photo together."*

In response, Edmund Bartlett, the Jamaican Tourism Minister, publicly thanked Tijana Kawashima Stojkovic in an event held at the country's embassy in Tokyo. The Minister said.

> *"Indeed, in a world that is often unabated by negatives, it is always refreshing when we experience random acts of kindness…I salute you Ms. Kawashima. You'll forever be etched in the hallowed halls of Jamaica's athletic history because you helped the outcome which led to the Gold Medal"*

As a reward for assisting the Olympian Hurdler to arrive at the National Stadium on time for the semifinals of the men's 110-meter hurdles of August 4, 2021, the Minister extended *Stojkovic* an all-expense paid package to visit famous Jamaican Tourists spots. This gesture was endorsed on social media by Prime Minister, Andrew Holness who succinctly shared that *"Every Jamaican knows that gratitude is a must"*

## JAMAICAN INDEPENDENCE CELEBRATIONS

The atmosphere of the entire Island exuded joy, hope and thanksgiving on the day of Jamaica's 59th Independence Celebrations, August 6, 2021. Elders told their young ones about the meaning of Independence, recounting the victory of leaving behind past colonial status and claiming rites as an Independent Nation.

Stories were told of the 'Glory Days' between 1962 through the early 1980's, when the Jamaican dollar was the strongest in the region and devaluation of the dollar was unheard of.

The introduction of the National Anthem, the National Pledge and the visit of Princess Margaret who represented the Queen of England to Jamaica were all significant features in the celebrations.

Many remembered the night at the Jamaican National Stadium on Arthur Wint Drive, Kingston Jamaica, when the British flag was lowered, lights turned off at 11.59 pm; lights turned on again at 12.01 am to mark the beginning of an era day. The Jamaican flag was raised for the first time, followed by the singing of the new National Anthem, *"Eternal Father Bless our Land, Guide us with Thy Mighty Hand,"* replacing the British Anthem *"God Save our Gracious Queen."*

New beginnings generated new activities at every level during the Independence celebrations. Over the years, Primary schools island-wide, participated in Festival of Arts activities, competing in oratory, music, poetry and art competitions, to triumphantly bring home medals awarded to the winners, annually.

Parades of the winners of Beauty Contests pageants were aired and displayed in the 3 Jamaican counties: Cornwall, Middlesex and Surrey, and also at the main cities, Kingston, Mandeville and Montego Bay.

The winner of the annual Festival Song contest was unveiled, and the new song could be heard all throughout the island, as it received maximum air play on all radio stations. The entire island resonated with joyful sounds deemed appropriate for the day's celebrations. Traditionally, radio stations played Jamaica Festival songs ranging from the early years through to the current winning song; a tradition started in 1966-present.

See complete listing: *Wikipedia. Popular Song Competition* (2022)

- 1966 - The Maytals with "Bam Bam"
- 1967 - The Jamaicans with "Ba, Ba Boom"
- 1968 - Desmond Dekker & The Aces with "Music Like Dirt (Intensified '68)"
- 1969 - The Maytals with "Sweet and Dandy"
- 1970 - Hopeton Lewis with "Boom Shacka Lacka"
- 1971 - Eric Donaldson with "Cherry Oh Baby"
- 1972 - Toots & the Maytals with "Pomps and Pride"
- 1973 - Marvin Brooks with "Jump In The Line"
- 1974 - Tinga Stewart with "Play de Music"
- 1975 - Roman Stewart with "Hooray Festival"
- 1976 - Freddie McKay with "Dance This Ya Festival"
- 1977 - Eric Donaldson with "Sweet Jamaica"
- 1978 - Eric Donaldson with "Land of my Birth"
- 1979 - The Astronauts with "Born Jamaican"
- 1980 - Stanley & The Turbines with "Come Sing With Me"
- 1981 - Tinga Stewart with "Nuh Wey Nuh Betta Dan Yard"
- 1982 - The Astronauts with "Mek Wi Jam"
- 1983 - Ras Karbi with "Jamaica I'll Never Leave You"
- 1984 - Eric Donaldson with "Proud to be Jamaican"
- 1985 - Roy Rayon with "Love Fever"
- 1986 - Stanley & The Turbines with "Dem a fe Squirm"
- 1987 - Roy Rayon with "Give Thanks and Praise"
- 1988 - Singer Jay with "Jamaica Land We Love"
- 1989 - Michael Forbes with "Stop and Go"
- 1990 - Robbie Forbes with "Island Festival"
- 1991 - Roy Rayon with "Come Rock"
- 1992 - Heather Grant with "Mek wi Put Things Right"
- 1993 - Eric Donaldson with "Big It Up"
- 1994 - Stanley & The Astronauts with "Dem a Pollute"
- 1995 - Eric Donaldson with "Join de Line"

- 1996 - Zac Henry & Donald White with "Meck We Go Spree"
- 1997 - Eric Donaldson with "Peace and Love"
- 1998 - Neville Martin with "Jamaica Whoa"
- 1999 - Cheryl Clarke with "Born Inna JA"
- 2000 - Stanley Beckford with "Fi Wi Island A Boom"
- 2001 - Roy Richards with "Lift Up Jamaica"
- 2002 - Devon Black with "Progress"
- 2003 - Stefan Penicillin with "Jamaican Tour Guide"
- 2004 - Stefan Penicillin with "Ole Time Jamaica"
- 2005 - Khalil N Pure with "Poverty"
- 2006 - Omar Reid with "Remember the Days"
- 2007 - Neville 'Gunty' Winters with "Woman A Di Beauty"
- 2008 - Roy Rayon with "Rise and Shine"
- 2009 - Winston Hussey with "Take Back Jamaica"
- 2010 - Kharuso with "My Jamaica"
- 2011 - Everton David Pessoa with "Oh if We"
- 2012 - Abbygaye Dallas with "Real Born Jamaican"
- 2013 - The competition was not held in 2013
- 2014 - Rushane Sanderson with "I Love JA"
- 2015 - Lee-Roy Johnson with "Celebration"
- 2016 - O'Neil Scott with "No Weh Like Jamaica"
- 2017 - The competition was not held in 2017
- 2018 - O'Neil 'Nazzle Man' Scott with "Jamaica A Wi Home"
- 2019 - Raldene Dyer with "Loaded Eagle"
- 2020 - Buju Banton with "I am a Jamaican"
- 2021 - Stacious with "Jamaican Spirit"
- 2022 - Sacaj with "Nuh Weh Nice Like Yard"
- 2023 – Slashe with "Best in the World

An annual National Service Awards event has been a traditional feature of the Independence celebrations. Distinguished services are awarded to Jamaicans in every sector of the nation, presented by the Governor General of Jamaica. The award ceremony and Grand Gala are traditionally held on the grounds of Kings' House, followed by the grand finale, The Governor Generals' Ball, a formal occasion where recipients and invited guests wearing ultra-modern attires are photographed and published in leading magazines to be admired by all, the next day.

Members of Maxine's community, sitting on the verandah, watching the events of the day unfold on the big-screen television, were visibly emotional. It was a fitting end to a momentous day, as they reflected on the journey that brought them together as a nation, sustained them through hardship and inspired Jamaica to greatness. The love of country transcended all other emotions and it was a surreal moment, as in unison, the gathering on the verandah sang the National Pledge of Jamaica, a patriotic song written by Victor Stafford Reid with music by Gustav Holst.

> *"I pledge my heart forever to serve with humble pride, this shining homeland ever, so long as earth abide.*
>
> *I pledge my heart this island, as God and faith shall live. My work, my strength, my love and my loyalty to give.*
>
> *Oh, green isle of the Indies, Jamaica strong and free. Our vows and loyal promises, Oh, heartland 'tis to thee."*

## MEMORIES OF 1962 JAMAICA INDEPENDENCE CELEBRATIONS

1962: Guests in the main stand at the National Stadium rise at midnight in salute to the Jamaica National Flag as it was raised to the top of the flagstaff during the ceremonies celebrating Jamaica's Independence. At right center Princess Margaret and the Earl of Snowdon stand in the Royal Box. The Princess with eyes raised to the flag.

COURTESY OF THE JAMAICA GLEANER

**1962 Celebrations: Children celebrated at a treat given by the Custos of St. Andrew, the Hon. A Russell Graham at his home on Birdsucker Lane, St. Andrew. The group of over five hundred children danced, sang, watched cowboy films and enjoyed ice cream, fudge, and many other treats.**

COURTESY OF THE JAMAICA GLEANER

(c) 1962 The Gleaner Co. (Media) Ltd.

**A boy sells mini Jamaican flags in Kingston, days before the country is officially declared independent. "TIME FOR FLAGS" called the youngster, in downtown Kingston.**

COURTESY OF THE JAMAICA DAILY GLEANER

*Maureen Bourne Linton and J. Robert Linton*

# CHAPTER 3

# SOAR

*"Bang" goes the starters gun. A clear command to soar.*
*The runner exhales; runs out of the block; not jumping; initially accelerating to top speed. Once top speed is achieved, endurance kicks in. Runner tries to maintain top speed for the rest of the journey.*

## Suddenly COVID: The proverbial '*Agony of Defeat*'

Mysteriously and without prior warning signs, grave illnesses and death tolls started to rise in the small community of Bell Blossoms and neighboring villages. The thrill of victory and the glory days suddenly came to a grinding halt.

News travelled at lightning speed and the calamity, which was first announced to be happening island wide, was revealed as a global crisis. However, no one could give a proper accounting of the source of this mystery.

The first clue came in from a foreign news report on January 9, 2020, via *CBS Morning News,* reported by *Anne-Marie Green.*

*"A new virus, related to Severe Acute Respiratory Syndrome (SARS) that was possibly responsible for a mysterious pneumonia outbreak in China: The new coronavirus was found in 15 of 59 patients with the illness. The virus is spread through coughing or sneezing or by touching an infected person."*

This was the introduction of the cataclysmic COVID, an unpresidential virus of Biblical proportion. In adherence to the laws of the World Health

Organization (WHO), all faces had to be covered with masks of all descriptions. According to reports received from international sources, life everywhere had changed dramatically and life in the village became somber. News of the loss of lives of friends and relatives from other places on the island, and also friends and relatives living abroad poured into the Bell Blossoms.

Eldith constantly gathered news from neighboring villages, on the subject, and her constant cries of Death, added to the deep despair which hung over the village.

All schools island wide remained closed after the Christmas break. Attempts to maintain Online classes were challenging, due to unstable WIFI delivery. At first, students actively connected by texting and phone calls, however, connections diminished as the demands of caring for family members and the mourning for loss of lives overwhelmed the society.

All sport and game activities, both nationally and internationally, were suspended, as "Distancing" became the new norm. Maxine, Marty, Barry along with other surviving villagers spent most of their mask-covered days caring for loved ones in the community.

It was evident that Myra Bennett's struggles with pre-existing health conditions had weakened her resistance, making her a prime target for COVID. She developed spells of uncontrollable coughing and congestion; therefore, she was tested for the virus. Unfortunately, her result was positive and she was immediately quarantined.

Barry had been very attentive to her, as his flexible work schedule made it possible. He silently grieved for Myra, and determined in his heart that he was fully prepared to do whatever was needed to keep her well. Unfortunately, headaches and a very high body temperature forced Barry to be tested also. His positive results for COVID further dampened the spirits of the entire community. Many prayers were sent up for both Barry and Myra. Unfortunately, within one week, both Myra and Barry passed away.

The shock of the precious losses numbed the village to contemplative silence. Marty was inconsolable as he reflected on the comradery he enjoyed with Barry, when they worked tirelessly on fun, sports-promotional programs. He reflected on Barry's contributions to the nation in all things, sports; the priceless time they spent together communicating with neighbors on the verandah; and the celebrations of glorious victories. Marty retreated to his room and mourned deeply.

Thankfully, Aunt Angela, Uncle Jim and family, stepped in and gave the support which was overwhelmingly needed during those dark days. Their contributions made a tremendous difference, as they strategically organized and made critical decisions.

Their little ones, Marlene and Mike, were helpful too, as they were always willing to run errands and eagerly did whatever tasks were assigned, without complaints.

Quickly seizing up the impact of the dilemma having of two deaths in one family, and under very strained COVID laws, Angela and Jim, made arrangements with the pastor for the commitment of both bodies in one combined service. Thankfully, all the relatives accepted the decision, ant it became easier for the neighbors, marshalled by Angela, to get all the details in place, while carefully distancing to prevent further loss of lives.

The Bennetts realized that funeral attendance would be impacted by the new normal of 'Distancing' imposed by the government under WHO guidelines, in response to the deadly nature of the disease. Marty shuddered to think of the very small attendance of fifteen loved ones who were permitted to attend the funeral service of Barry who contributed so much to his community. Maxine was saddened as she reflected on the outpouring of love her mother received in earlier days, when she initially suffered the stroke, in comparison to the limited number of attendees that would be allowed to attend the burial.

Both Maxine and Marty were challenged to soar; to learn more about Online and Social Media outreach. They researched and found that Zoom would be the best way to engage a wider audience at the actual service. It was evident that the world had changed and the fifteen people at the service were thrilled to be joined by hundreds of attendees by Zoom, as the Pastor addressed and solicited responses from both sets of participants.

Based on constant breaking news announcements of massive loss of lives, it finally dawned on the people of Bell Blossoms that in comparison, they were blessed to have lost only two from the Bell Blossoms community. Comforting words from the Pastor was well received by all, and the congregation lustily sang the hymn, *"Amazing Grace how sweet the sound,"* with the knowledge that their lives had been speared.

## FIRST EVIDENCE OF A COVID DEATH IN JAMAICA.

COURTESY OF THE JAMAICA GLEANER

First COVID death in Jamaica: Members of the Ministry of Health and Wellness and the Jamaica Constabulary Force visit the 79 year old male patient, marking the first COVID-19 related death in Jamaica.

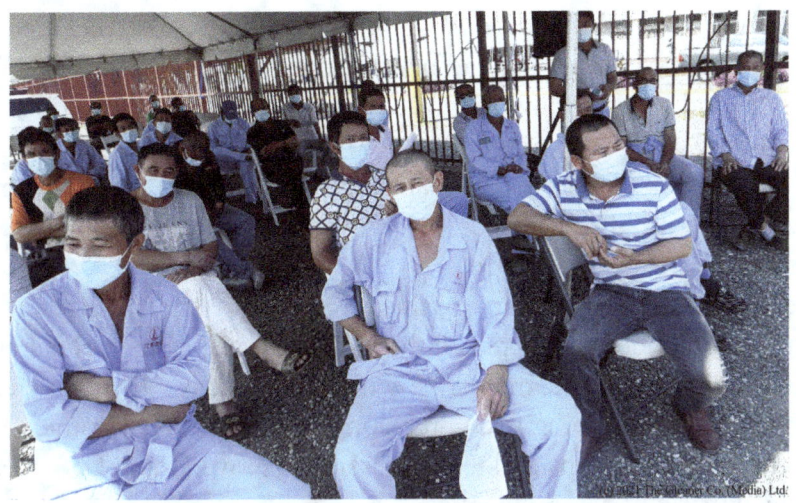

**Masked and Somber**

COURTESY OF THE JAMACA GLEANER

## THE EFFECTS OF COVID AND WORLD HEALTH ORGANIZATION (WHO) MANDATES ON ATHLETIC ACTIVITIES, 2020

Worldwide Olympic activities were severely affected by COVID, and in 2020 the Olympics was cancelled altogether. However, in 2021 limited forms of activities took place in Tokyo, Japan, between July 23rd through August 8th. The 2021 Olympics became controversial as the presence of spectators was limited, and global protests were raised. The lack of supporting fans negatively impacted other international games including the Diamond League in Europe; Premier League in UK; Tennis US Open; and Wimbledon Tennis Tournament in London.

Competitive events held without the loving support of fans in the stands were dreary. Gone were the uplifting and encouraging roars and cheers, celebratory colors, foods and smells. The power of the fans was severely tested, as an underlying fear of catching the deadly COVID virus prevailed. According to the Jamaican local evening news (2020),

*"Athletes, like well-trained soldiers, continued to compete under strange conditions, hoping for better days to come"*

Heavily imposed mandates did not go without the strong rebuttal of global freedom-seekers demanding fairness, justice and equity. WHO guidelines and other worldwide, governmental mandates were enforced for public safety and more importantly, to save lives. Mandates included curfews, vaccines, boosters, distancing and rigidly imposed masks. However, the steady resistance, or counterbalance of freedom seekers, created the perfect global storm.

New formats for worship, businesses, schools and colleges among myriads of other entities recreated their delivery, as business closures and working from home, became the new order of the day. With the creation of schooling, worshipping and conducting businesses from home, Online platforms such as Zooms and teleconferencing moved into place, creating a changed world of communication.

## HOPE AND RESILIENCE UPLIFTING THE HUMAN SPIRIT

Between 2021-2022, winds of change were gradually felt, and healing started to take place, based on many factors, including worldwide vaccinations; virus mutations; alongside the continual prayers for mercy and healing from the peoples of all tribes and nations of the world.

# THE BEAUTY OF THE ISLES BRINGS TRANQUILITY TO INSPIRE HOPE AND HEALING FROM THE ONSLAUGHT OF COVID

COURTESY OF BEVON ANGUS

Jamaica experienced an outpouring of neighborly care and kindness within the communities, as well as help from hospitals and global donor organizations. In 2022, death tolls increasingly fell nationally and internationally as the transient mutated virus was replaced by weaker strains marked by lessened hospitalizations and deaths.

In Bell Blossoms, the confidence level of the people began to return, and masks were slowly and cautiously removed. Ominous cries from Eldith subsided, as announcements of worldwide deaths of loved ones decreased. Throughout the entire saga, Eldith's jarring bellow added to the distress; however, her silence signaled hope. Sounds of normal life returned; children playing; balls bouncing; vendors scurrying; airplanes flying overhead; and the sound of traffic returning to normal, indicating the return of hope in the hearts of the people.

Businesses relevant to Jamaica including shipping and tourism, which is the nations' financial lifeblood, showed hopeful signs of upturn. Like petals unfolding, national and international reopening of the National Stadium, airports and other businesses slowly returned. The realization dawned on the people of Bell Blossoms that the majority of the world's population was finally recovering from COVID. Hopeful sparks of life began to glow as the world took on a new outlook. Eventually, glimmers of hope and resilience uplifted the human spirit.

Alexander Pope (1734) describes this best, in his essay on Man, *"Hope Springs Eternal in the Human Breast."*

## VALIDATION OF SPORTS AS A MENTORING TOOL

Maxine and Marty had mourned their losses and also felt encouraged by the renewed signs of life and healing in Bell Blossoms, their local community. Vendors returned to the marketplace; schools were partially opened; and some churches held Sunday services. Congregants were visibly emotional as they lustily sang the old hymn, *"Amazing Grace"* and gave thanks for the lives that were speared.

**2021 Olympics, Tokyo Japan:** Despite the ravishes of COVID and the lock-out of fans in the stands, the Olympic committee decided to hold the Olympics, under much protest from the sports community. As public gatherings were still outlawed, the gathering on the verandah did not take place. However, regardless of the climate, the Jamaican ladies, Elaine Thompson-Herah, Shelley Anne Fraser-Pryce, and Sherika Jackson, continued their stellar performance and celebrated another memorable Sweep in Tokyo, Japan, in the Women's 100 meters. These three ladies, already memorialized as legendary athletes of world class fame, motivated the world and in response, the people of Jamaica sincerely love them, and constantly cheer them on.

**2022-World Athletic Championship, Eugene, Oregon.** This event marked the first community gathering after COVID. Marty and Maxine were motivated to harness the true spirit of sportsmanship; set up the verandah chairs again, and turn on the big-screen television. They were happy to invite the community to join them in viewing the World Athletic Championship 2022, held in Eugene, Oregon.

The atmosphere was tense as the gathering swelled, heightened by the celebration of the 60th Anniversary of Jamaican Independence. Finally, a hush fell over the excited crowd as they awaited the loud explosion of the starter gun. The world watched in awe as the legendary athletes Shelly Anne Fraser-Pryce, Sherika Jackson and Elaine Thompson, for the third time in sports history, victoriously claimed another "Sweep" in the Women's' 100-meter finals. Shelley Ann Fraser-Pryce won the gold medal; Shericka Jackson, the silver; and Elaine Thompson Herah the bronze. This was a fitting 60th Anniversary gift to the people of Jamaica as they approached another Independence Celebration.

COURTESY OF JAMAICA GLEANER

**SWEEP – 2021: Women's 100m finals in Tokyo, Japan. Elaine Thompson-Herah, gold; Shelly Ann Fraser-Pryce, silver; and Shericka Jackson, bronze.**

COURTESY OF JAMAICA GLEANER

**Historic SWEEP of 2012: Men's 200 meter, London 2012; Usain Bolt (center) gold , Yohan Blake (left) silver and Warren Weir (right) bronze**

The victory of the Athletes sent deep and significant messages to people everywhere. Maxine took this as a personal victory, which validated her resolve to achieve her chosen lifelong goal to become a doctor and the very best doctor in her field of Pediatric Surgery.

Marty extensively broadcasted plans to make an outstanding homecoming celebrations for the athletes returning to the Island of Jamaica.

Mr. MacLean felt the urgency of his message to his protégées. He had a classroom of students to motivate; to achieve their highest potentials. Armed with legendary stories of the famous Ninth Street Battle between King's High and Pope high school, he regaled his homeroom with stories of the euphoric 1965 championship, when King's High rose up and defeated the Pope giants, after 3 consecutive years of defeat. As always, he concluded with the resounding battle cry of King's High, *"Never yield, never give up."*

Mr. MacLean also reminded his protégées that the current victory was a reminder that moral standards were upheld, as the girls were thoroughly tested for banned substances after completing each race.

This standard was also demonstrated by Usain Bolt, *the fastest man on the planet* who faithfully tested negative for drugs and banned substances, thus upholding the standard for athletes everywhere. Ultimately, Jamaican teachers and parents are highly encouraged to continue to support and raise up true champions.

Maxine also remembered her last encounter with Eldith who knew of her plans to return to school.

"Poor little Prodigal," Eldith said in soft voice.

"You really plan to leave your loving community to wander into that big foreign world? Be careful!"

Maxine was visibly moved, as she had never before encountered Eldith's soft, and caring voice.

## WORK STUDY – A NOVEL CONCEPT

The unfolding events swirled in Maxine thoughts as she came to the end of her first year at Kent High in 2022. She reflected on one event in school, which highlighted how much she needed patience, discipline and diligence to soar to excellence.

She remembered her early days of impatience when she eagerly scanned the Work Study job boards occasionally to see assignments listed for the Biology lab. Although she was only a junior, she already knew where she wanted to work, based on her career choice, and she could not wait to get that opportunity to participate in the Kent High, Work Study program. Other students had the same idea and gradually, Work Study became a hot topic for discussion in her 7th Grade homeroom. Miss Dean thought her juniors were much too anxious, but they were not convinced, as many of them were sure that Work Study would present the perfect introduction to their chosen careers.

Maxine was especially impatient, as the structure of the science curriculum in the seventh grade did not offer her the opportunity she sought to explore. "A doctor must understand human sciences," she mused. Forms 1-3, general science curriculum with the focus on flora, fauna, and astronomy, was not what she envisioned in high school.

As the class gathered in the homeroom one morning, an appeal for volunteers was announced over the intercom. It was announced that a sharp Caribbean storm had ripped through the community on the weekend, uprooting trees and causing minor damage to some buildings. Unfortunately, heavy winds blew the door of the Biology lab wide open, knocking lab equipment off the shelves and toppling models of body parts. Posters and books were strewn all over the floor and broken jars presented quite the hazard. Although a team of professionals from a local Hazardous Waste company had completed the initial cleaning-up of the poisons and the shattered glass on the floor, help was needed to put the room together again, and restore wet printed materials.

Maxine was first in-line at the lab, as this was the opportunity she longed for. Unfortunately, as she stepped through the door, her curiosity got the better of her. Without waiting to follow critical instructions from the Biology teacher, Maxine, quite caught up in her career dreams, wandered off. She picked up instruments she recognized from the health magazines; leafed through wet pages of books illustrating parts of the human body; and became excited as she ran her hands over models of the human heart, lungs and other body parts.

Maxine, lost in her euphoric dreams, would have gone on forever in this new world of discovery, but the furious voice of Mr. Booth the Science Master caught her attention. He shouted at her to stop touching, and to wash her hands immediately. Quickly Maxine complied.

However, when she turned around the entire group of eight volunteers stared at her. She froze, feeling chills of embarrassment down her spine. Maxine suddenly realized she was way out of line. Mr. Booth explained that although the initial cleaning-up of the poisons and shattered glass in the room was done, this team of volunteers would be required to do a longer-term restoration job, as wet paper was a factor.

Mr. Booth distributed gloves and gave very precise and comprehensive directives, explaining the need to avoid any broken pieces of glass or the danger of touching contaminated water left over from the initial cleaners. Restoration required much patience, as the delicate task of rinsing and restoring all printed materials, including the posters which fell from the wall, books, magazines and transparencies, while avoiding any residue of remaining glass on the floor.

At the end of the session, Mr. Booth detained Maxine, giving her a full lecture on safety and the need to follow instructions. She was embarrassed but thankful that he allowed her to continue with the project. The work accomplished over the next week was amazing. Full restoration was accomplished, and the team was highly commended for their diligence in completing the task. Maxine learned the importance of being a collaborator. She discovered that greater success could be achieved with patience and diligence.

The team of eight bonded quite easily, as a result of working really hard, in close quarters for the duration of one week. They came from a range of classes between 7th-12th grade, and they all aspired to achieve science-based careers including botany, zoology, veterinary science, teaching science or medicine. Maxine was thrilled to have a set of friends with similar career interests in the field of science. This broadened her perspective of Kent High, and she easily interacted with them across campus, whether in her dormitory; at mealtimes in the cafeteria; on the playfield; or during after-school activities.

It was an amazing semester of innovative ideas. She compared Aunt Angela's experience of yesteryear to her current experiences and realized that rapid changes had taken place. Kent High, like the rest of the world, had to battle the ravishes of COVID to survive. Aunt Angela had educated her on the solid foundation of this institution, and this gave her a good sense of the direction the school would take, upon recovery. It was comforting to know that while COVID disrupted the flow, and put processes on pause, Kent High was poised for greatness and would survive and become even stronger. Maxine looked forward to being a part of the rebuilding efforts.

COURTESY OF BEVON ANGUS
**Calm after a stormy semester**

## RETURNING HOME

At the end of the semester, Maxine got off the bus and headed towards home, hoping to get inside unnoticed. However, she ran into Eldith, who made such a racket.

"The Prodigal has come home, the Prodigal has come home!" she yelled, practically dancing in the street. Maxine smiled, fully grasping that Eldith, in her strange way, was expressing her love. It was good to be home.

Maxine was never athletic, and Kent, her chosen high school, was never outstanding in sport competitions; however, the athletic victories that permeated the Jamaican society became a part of everyone' life. It is remarkable to experience how the constant tensions between victory and defeat in athletics, validate the resilience of the human spirit. Crowning moments of triumph had far-reaching effects to uplift, motivate and boost morale, even as the world continued to battle the agonies and despair of lingering, residual COVID.

The recent post-COVID victories demonstrate the resilience of the track team to the community of Bell Blossoms and the faithful fans who gather on the verandah to celebrate the most recent "2022, Sweep" in Eugene, Oregon. The victory signified the nation's recovery and the strategy to continue to hold up the standard of world-class athleticism. It is heartening to see how the global sports community continued to embrace the thrill of victory; and the legendary girls continue to inspire people everywhere to achieve greater victories regardless of the circumstances.

## 2023: CONTINUATION OF THE WINNING STREAK IN BUDAPEST

Regardless of the circumstances, the Jamaican athletic community continue to strive relentlessly for success. August 24th was declared Jamaica Day by Sports Commentators at the 2023 World Athletic Championship, in Budapest, Hungary.

(See table of *2023 – World Athletic Championship, Hungary on page 66*)

In the afternoon of Wednesday, August 24th, Jamaica won five medals. In Long Jump, Wayne Pinnock won silver and Tajah Gayle won bronze, while another Jamaica was placed 4th.

Later that day, Danielle Williams won gold in the 110-meter hurdles. Also, Antonio Watson won a great victory in the men's 400-meters and became the first Jamaican to win a 400-meter gold medal in 40 years, which was won by Bert Cameron in 1983. On the same day, Rushell Clayton also claimed a bronze medal in the women's 400-meter hurdles. Over the duration of the games, August 19 - 27, Jamaica won a total of 12 medals, claiming 3 golds, 4 silvers, and 5 bronze.

Earlier, Shericka Jackson got a silver medal in 100-meter and Shelly-Ann Fraser-Pryce got Bronze in the 100- meter. Ainsley Parchment also received a silver medal in the 110-meter Hurdles. Sherika Jackson won the 200-meter gold in 20.41 seconds, claiming the 2nd fastest time in history after Flo Jo, in 1988. Continuing the winning streak, on Friday August 26, 2023, the women's 4x100-meter relay team claimed a silver medal, and the men's 4x100-meter relay team claimed a bronze medal.

(c) 2019 The Gleaner Co. (Media) Ltd.

COURTESY OF THE JAMAICA GLEANER
**Legendary Sprinter - Shelley-Ann Fraser-Pryce**

Kudos to Shelley-Ann Fraser-Pryce, winner of a silver medal in the 4x100-meter relay in, perhaps her final World Athletic Championship games. The Legendary Shelley, affectionately called 'Mama Rocket,' has accumulated a total of 17 medals from World Championships, over the years.

# 2023 – RESULTS OF THE WORLD ATHLETIC CHAMPIONSHIP, HUNGARY

| NAME | MEDAL | EVENT |
|---|---|---|
| Shericka Jackson | Silver | Women's 100 meters |
| Shelly-Ann Fraser-Pryce | Bronze | Women's 100 meters |
| Ainsley Parchment | Silver | 110 meters hurdles |
| Pinnock Wayne | Silver | Men's Long Jump |
| Tajah Gayle | Bronze | Men's Long Jump |
| Danielle Williams | Gold | Women's 110 meters hurdles |
| Antonio Watson | Gold | Men's 400 meters hurdles |
| Rushell Clayton | Bronze | Women's 400 meters hurdles |
| Shericka Jackson | Gold | Women's 200 meters |
| | | |
| -Shashalee Forbes<br>-Shelly-Ann Fraser-Pryce<br>-Shericka Jackson<br>-Natasha Morrison<br>-Elaine Thompson-Herah<br>-Briana Williams | Silver | Women's 4 × 100 meters relay |
| Candice McLeod<br>Nickisha Pryce<br>Janieve Russell<br>Shiann Salmon<br>Ronda Whyte<br>Charokee Young | Silver | Women's 4 × 400 meters relay |
| Ackeem Blake<br>Ryiem Forde<br>Oblique Seville<br>Rohan Watson | Bronze | Men's 4 × 100 meters relay |

Victory was confirmed by the resounding cheers from the people on the verandah, which was heard, echoing across the community of Bell Blossoms, and revibrated over the mountains and valleys of Jamaica.

"Ready, set, soar!" Maxine mused to herself. In her heart she knew that the grimness imposed by the COVID experience also factored in building her resolve to strive for success. In aspiring to soar, she learned that soaring did not guarantee a smooth ride. Each experience heightened her awareness of the journey and gave her the confidence needed to take each necessary step forward. As an overcomer she had endured character-building, life-changing experiences, which would take her through high school and through college to achieve her goals.

Maxine's reoccurring dreams of her future as a Pediatric Surgeon continued over the years. For this, Maxine was thankful as it kept her focused, and she was thrilled by the thought of someday achieving her lifelong dream of establishing a Health Care Center in Bell Blossoms District, Jamaica, West Indies.

Maxine continues to rise early in the morning to enjoy the beautiful sunrise of hope, overlooking the Bell Blossoms hills. Today, she remembers one of the favorite hymns sung during the burials of the COVID victims, *"Amazing Grace."* Feeling thankful and fully motivated, she quietly voiced the last verse of the song.

> *"Through many dangers, toils and snares we have already come, Tis Grace that's brought us safe thus far and Grace will lead us home."*

# NATURAL, INSPIRING LANDSCAPE OF HOPE

COURTESY OF CHRISTOPHER KELMAN

COURTESY OF CHRISTOPHER KELMAN

*Maureen Bourne Linton and J. Robert Linton*

# REFERENCES

Bertram, Arnold (2016)"NW Manly and the Making of Modern Jamaica." Arawak Publications, Jamaica.

Bolt, Usain. (2016) The Fastest Man Alive: The Story of Usain Bolt Harper Collins Publishers Limited, NY

Cash, Meredith. (2021) Jamaican Hurdler Hansle Parchment The Business Insider, India Times Internet Limited (TIL) India

Fabisch, Pablo E. (2005) Telemachus and Mentor (1699 Image)

http://paesmem.stanford.edu/html/proceedings_4.html

Green, Anne-Marie, COVID Report, CBS Morning News, January 9, 2020

Grant, Michael A., Lawrence, Hubert. (2012) The Power & the Glory: Jamaica in World Athletics, from WWII to the Diamond League Era Great House publishing, Kingston Communications, Kingston, Jamaica W.I.

Jessie Owens' Inspiring History - Olympics https://olympics.com/en/video/jesse-owens-s-inspiring-history, Retrieved 10/8/2022

Kracov Julie, *CBS, Year in Review: Top News Stories of 2020, December 27, 2020.*

Linton, M. (2022) Postal Workers Interviews, Mile Gully, Walderstand and Kingston, Jamaica

National Today. Bonfire Night - When is it? What's the best way to celebrate? Nov 5, 2023 https://nationaltoday.com, Retrieved 3/27/23

Pope, Alexander(1734) Man

Rhodes, Jean (2001) Mentorship https://en.wikipedia.org/wiki/Mentor_(Odyssey) Wikipedia. Veronica Campbell Brown, (2021).
https://en.wikipedia.org/wiki/Veronica_Campbell_Brown, Retrieved September 2021

Wikipedia. Popular Song Competition.
https://en.wikipedia.org/wiki/Jamaica_Independence_Festival#cite_note-8
Retrieved April 2023

Yendi Phillips, You tube Interview, Usain Bolt, (2021)

Yendi Phillips, You tube Interview, Shelley Anne Frazier-Pryce, (2020)

Yendi Phillips, You tube Interviews, Elaine Thompson-Herrah, (2021)

Yendi Phillips, You tube Interviews, Sherika Jackson, (2021)

Wikipedia, Jamaica at the 2023 World Athletics Championships (2023)
https://en.wikipedia.org/wiki/Jamaica_at_the_2023_World_Athletics_Championships
Retrieved 8/27/23

advbookstore.com